Dear Parents:

Congratulations! Your child is taking the first steps on an exciting journey. The destination? Independent reading!

STEP INTO READING® will help your child get there. The program offers five steps to reading success. Each step includes fun stories and colorful art or photographs. In addition to original fiction and books with favorite characters, there are Step into Reading Non-Fiction Readers, Phonics Readers and Boxed Sets, Sticker Readers, and Comic Readers—a complete literacy program with something to interest every child.

Learning to Read, Step by Step!

Ready to Read Preschool–Kindergarten
• big type and easy words • rhyme and rhythm • picture clues
For children who know the alphabet and are eager to begin reading.

Reading with Help Preschool–Grade 1
• basic vocabulary • short sentences • simple stories
For children who recognize familiar words and sound out new words with help.

Reading on Your Own Grades 1–3
• engaging characters • easy-to-follow plots • popular topics
For children who are ready to read on their own.

Reading Paragraphs Grades 2–3
• challenging vocabulary • short paragraphs • exciting stories
For newly independent readers who read simple sentences with confidence.

Ready for Chapters Grades 2–4
• chapters • longer paragraphs • full-color art
For children who want to take the plunge into chapter books but still like colorful pictures.

STEP INTO READING® is designed to give every child a successful reading experience. The grade levels are only guides; children will progress through the steps at their own speed, developing confidence in their reading. The F&P Text Level on the back cover serves as another tool to help you choose the right book for your child.

Remember, a lifetime love of reading starts with a single step!

To Della, Leo, and Abe,
with love
—M.B.

To my fiercest
dog-loving sister, Jennie
—H.H.

Text copyright © 2017 by Maribeth Boelts
Cover art and interior illustrations copyright © 2017 by Hollie Hibbert

Visit us on the Web!
StepIntoReading.com
randomhousekids.com

Educators and librarians, for a variety of teaching tools, visit us at RHTeachersLibrarians.com

Library of Congress Cataloging-in-Publication Data
Names: Boelts, Maribeth, author. | Hibbert, Hollie, illustrator.
Title: The fairy dogmother / Maribeth Boelts, Hollie Hibbert.
Description: First edition. | New York : Random House, [2017] | Series: Step into reading.
Step 3 | Summary: Fairy Godmother teaches young fairies—and Ivy the dog—to become fairy godmothers, but something is missing.
Identifiers: LCCN 2016018409 (print) | LCCN 2016033930 (ebook) |
ISBN 978-1-101-93446-3 (paperback) | ISBN 978-1-101-93450-0 (lib. bdg.) |
ISBN 978-1-101-93451-7 (ebook)
Subjects: | CYAC: Dogs—Fiction. | Fairy godmothers—Fiction. | Fairies—Fiction. | Magic—Fiction. Classification: LCC PZ8.B6375 Fai 2017 (print) | LCC PZ8.B6375 (ebook) | DDC [E]—dc23

Printed in the United States of America
10 9 8 7 6 5 4 3 2 1

This book has been officially leveled by using the F&P Text Level Gradient™ Leveling System.

The Fairy Dogmother

by Maribeth Boelts

illustrated by Hollie Hibbert

Random House New York

Once upon a time,
there was a lonely dog
without a home.
Fairy Godmother found her
hiding in the ivy.
"I have a home
without a dog," she said.
"Would you like to come
live with me?"

Fairy Godmother
named the dog Ivy.
She thought Ivy was
a simple dog.
She taught her simple tricks.

"Sit, Ivy,"

said Fairy Godmother.

And Ivy sat.

"Stay, Ivy,"

said Fairy Godmother.

And Ivy stayed.

"Good dog!"

said Fairy Godmother.

But Ivy knew she could
do much more than
sit and stay.

One day,

Fairy Godmother said,

"I am old.

I need to teach young fairies

how to be fairy godmothers."

Ivy wagged her tail.

Could she learn, too?

Fairies flew on the

backs of dragonflies

to Fairy Godmother's house.

The class began.

Ivy watched every move.

"Our first lesson

is waving magic wands,"

said Fairy Godmother.

All the fairies

waved their wands.

"Our second lesson
is clicking heels,"
said Fairy Godmother.
All the fairies
clicked their heels.

"Our third lesson
is singing sweet songs,"
said Fairy Godmother.
All the fairies
sang sweet songs.

The fairies waved,

clicked,

and sang their best.

There were sparks.

There were sputters.

But no magic appeared.

Fairy Godmother
scratched her head.
"I must be doing
something wrong,"
she said.

"Let's try flying lessons.
Fairy godmothers
must know how to fly."
The fairies climbed
Fairy Godmother's
tallest tree.
"One, two, three . . .
JUMP!" she said.

Plop!

The fairies landed in a heap.

"Oh, dear!"

said Fairy Godmother.

"What am I forgetting?"

When the lesson was over,

Fairy Godmother and Ivy

walked to the library.

Fairy Godmother searched

books for an answer.

Ivy peeked out the window.

Just then,
she saw a young maiden
trip and fall
into a mud puddle.

Ker-plop!

Her basket tipped over,

and her dress tore.

Ivy grabbed

Fairy Godmother's wand.

She raced outside to help.

I'll try some magic,

she thought.

Ivy waved the wand.

Presto!

The maiden turned into

a mouse!

Whoops!

What if I click my claws?

thought Ivy.

Ivy clicked her claws.

The mouse turned into

a monkey!

Oh, no! thought Ivy.

Then Ivy howled

a sweet song.

The monkey covered its ears

and dashed around

the village square.

Fairy Godmother
heard the ruckus.
She left her books
and flew to Ivy.

The monkey jumped

into Fairy Godmother's arms.

It reached into her pocket.

It pulled out

a silver pouch.

"My fairy dust!"

said Fairy Godmother.

"That's what I forgot!

Now the magic will work!"

Fairy Godmother
opened her bag
of fairy dust.
"Your heart is so kind, Ivy.
You get the first sprinkle."

Fairy Godmother
sprinkled Ivy
from head to tail.
Ivy's fur turned
a pretty purple.
She began to float.
"I can fly!" said Ivy.
"And I can speak!"

Then Fairy Godmother
gave Ivy her own
magic wand.

Ivy waved the wand
over the monkey.
The monkey turned into
a mouse!

Ivy clicked her claws.
The mouse turned into
a muddy maiden!

Then Ivy howled
a really sweet song.

Just like that,

the basket and dress

were as good as new!

The tidy maiden skipped away.

"Thank you!" she said.

"I did it!" said Ivy.

"I must find others

who need a fairy godmother."

Ivy flew off,

searching high and low.

She spotted a skinny dog.

The dog was begging

for a bone

at the butcher shop.

But the butcher

shooed him away.

"Poor dog," said Ivy.

She swooped down.

The skinny dog trembled.

"Don't be afraid," said Ivy.

She waved her wand.

A juicy steak appeared

in a brand-new bowl.

"That's not all," said Ivy.

She clicked her claws.

A soft, warm bed appeared.

The skinny dog
ate the steak and
plopped down in the bed.

"My work is done," said Ivy.

She gave the dog

a pat on the head.

But he whimpered.

"You had a steak," said Ivy.

The skinny dog

whimpered again.

"You have a soft bed,"

said Ivy.

Then she remembered

something.

She used to be a lonely dog.

Fairy Godmother took her in.

"I know what you are
missing!" she said.
"But this will take
a lot of magic."

Then Ivy howled
her sweetest song yet.
Glass cracked.
Babies cried.

The skinny dog
covered his ears.

Suddenly,

a boy appeared!

He bent down to pet

the skinny dog.

The dog gave him a lick.

"You just needed a friend,"

said Ivy.

"Woof!" agreed

the skinny dog.

Ivy knew right then
she wasn't a
fairy godmother.
She was a fairy *dogmother.*
And she could make
any dog's wishes
come true!